To Marc, Yuna and Adriel.

Susanna Isern

To Viola.

Marco Somá

nubeclassics

Dormouse and his Seven Beds
Nubeclassics Series

© Text: Susanna Isern, 2017
© Illustrations: Marco Somá, 2017
© Edition: NubeOcho, 2017
www.nubeocho.com - hello@nubeocho.com

Original title: *Las siete camas de Lirón*
Translator: Ben Dawlatly
Text editing: Rebecca Packard

Distributed in the United States by
Consortium Book Sales & Distribution

First edition: 2018
ISBN: 978-84-946926-6-6

Printed in China by KS Printing,
respecting international labor standards.

Dormouse and his Seven Beds

Susanna Isern   Marco Somà

nubeOCHO

The days in **Green Forest** were tranquil and uneventful, sometimes even verging on boring. The animals would eat berries, stroll through the meadows, cool off in the lake, jump from branch to branch and nap in the shade of the trees.

But, that summer, **something unexpected** started to happen in some of the houses in Green Forest.

Rabbit was the first to notice. As dawn broke, he leaped out of bed and hopped over to prepare his breakfast. And he found little **Dormouse** peacefully sleeping in his **carrot box**.

"**Dormouse!** You gave me such a fright! What are you doing here?"

"Sorry, **Rabbit!** I couldn't get to sleep last night, so I thought I'd try a different **bed**."

The next morning, there was a similar surprise in **Robin's** house. He woke up feeling groggy, and when he went to freshen up, he found little **Dormouse** sleeping like a log in his **tie drawer**.

"Wake up, **Dormouse!** What are you doing in my house at this time of day?"

"My apologies, **Robin!** I couldn't get to sleep last night, so I thought I'd try a different **bed**."

Next it was **Deer's** turn. When he got out of bed, he noticed that one side of his head was heavier than the other. When he looked in the mirror, he saw little **Dormouse** curled up on **one of his antlers.**

"**Dormouse,** do you mind telling me why exactly you're on my head?"

"I'm so sorry, **Deer!** I couldn't get to sleep last night, so I thought I'd try a different bed."

It went on like this every night. Little **Dormouse** kept trying different beds and startling whoever found him in the **morning**.

Bear's shoe, **Tortoise's** glasses case,
Mouse's cuckoo clock, **Squirrel's**
music box...

One day, the animals got fed up with little **Dormouse** appearing tucked away in **unexpected** places in their **homes** every morning, so they decided to have a word with him.

"We're sorry, **Dormouse**. But it's just not okay for you to creep into our houses in the middle of the night. From now on, we think it's best for you to stay in your own bed," said **Rabbit**.

"But..." **Dormouse** started trying to explain.

"No buts and no ifs!" interrupted Tortoise. "I'm too old for such frights."

The next morning, **Green Forest** was back to normal: serene, and even a little boring. Little **Dormouse** did not wake up in anybody else's bed. **None of the animals even saw him all day.**

That evening, **Rabbit** went to visit him to see how he was. But the lights at Dormouse's house were out and the **front door** was **bolted** shut.

Owl lived next door to little **Dormouse**. She would stay awake at night keeping watch over the forest. **Rabbit** was worried, so he asked her about their little friend.

"Good evening, **Owl**. Have you seen **Dormouse**?"

"Last night I saw him leave with a suitcase."

"**Dormouse** has left the forest? But... why?"

"Oh, **Rabbit,** I thought you knew. **Dormouse** is really scared of sleeping alone."

Rabbit ran hastily through the trees to let the other animals know.

"Guys! Guys! Owl just told me that Dormouse has left Green Forest. Now I know why he used to come to our houses in the middle of the night... He's afraid of being alone at night."

"Oh, the poor thing!" they all said, full of shock and regret.

"But there's even worse news. Owl told me that she saw him heading toward Gray Forest."

The animals set off to look for him straightaway. The one and only terrifying **Wolf** lived in **Gray Forest**.

When they reached the **ferocious** animal's **lair**, they cautiously popped their noses in through the window. And there he was. They saw **Dormouse** calmly slumbering tucked into a giant sock. Nearby, **Wolf was snoring** in bed.

Rabbit snuck in through the window. He tip-toed over to little Dormouse and rescued him by dragging him out in the sock.

Once outside, Bear laid Dormouse gently on his head, and they all headed back to Green Forest together.

They arrived at sunrise. **Dormouse** yawned and rubbed his eyes.

"But... how did I end up here?" he asked when he saw everybody.

"You can thank us that you're safe and sound. What made you think it was a good idea to sleep at **Wolf's** place?" asked **Robin.**

"Well, I thought he wouldn't mind keeping me **company** at night..."

"You should have told us what was up. Don't worry, from now on you can **sleep with us.** We have a **plan!**" announced Rabbit.

From then on, little **Dormouse** spent each night in a different bed.

Mondays in **Rabbit's carrot** box, **Tuesdays** in **Robin's tie** drawer, **Wednesdays** on **Deer's** left **antler**, **Thursdays** in **Bear's shoe**, **Fridays** in **Tortoise's glasses** case, **Saturdays** in **Mouse's** cuckoo **clock**, and **Sundays** in **Squirrel's music** box.

In the company of his friends, **Dormouse** wasn't frightened, and he'd fall asleep in the blink of an eye.

One **Monday** morning, **Rabbit** woke up to find the **carrot** box **empty**.

Rabbit was worried, so he asked the other **animals** if Dormouse had spent the **night** at one of their houses, but none of them had seen him.

Rabbit ran to **Dormouse's** place to see if he was alright. He found him in his bed.

"Good morning, **Dormouse**. How are you? I thought you'd be spending the night in my **carrot box**."

"Shhhhh!" whispered Dormouse as he half opened his eyes. "You'll **wake her up!**"

And there at the end of his bed, peacefully sleeping, was his new friend, miniscule **Pygmy Shrew**.